D1214235

For Toby Silverton, Queen of Tea.
With special thanks to Jori van der Linde
for making magic from my words.

—Tiffany

To those who have shared with me
a lovely cup of tea.

—Jori

Published in 2015 by Simply Read Books
www.simplyreadbooks.com

Library and Archives Canada Cataloguing in Publication

Stone, Tiffany, 1967-, author
Teatime / written by Tiffany Stone ; illustrated by Jori van der Linde.

ISBN 978-1-927018-67-5 (bound)

I. Van der Linde, Jori, illustrator II. Title.

PS8637.T66T43 2015 jC813'.6 C2014-906179-X

We gratefully acknowledge for their financial support of our publishing program the Canada Council for the Arts, the BC Arts Council, and the Government of Canada through the Canada Book Fund (CBF).

Manufactured in Malaysia.
Book design by Heather Lohnes.
Typeset in Valentina typeface, designed by Pedro Arilla (CC BY-ND 3.0), with hand-drawn text by Jori van der Linde.

10 9 8 7 6 5 4 3 2 1

"May all
our dreams
be sweet
tonight."

we snuggle, cozy,
in our beds

and whisper
in the soft moonlight,

With berries
tucked

beneath our
heads,

The sun has set. It's getting late.

a playground that will have to wait.

The fun around us
never ends–
a playground for
two fairy friends–

tea

. . . a cake!

before
our feet
begin
to ache–

we jump up, up onto

We glide between
the cookie crumbs
and just before
we're cold and numb–

Around

and

'round

and

'round

we whirl.

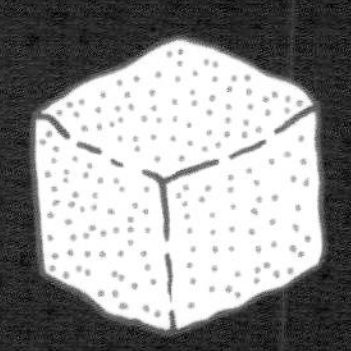

We twist and loop and lunge

and twirl.

a frozen
pond where
we can skate.

Till

plop

we

land

upon a plate,

I'll join you and we'll
both climb out

by sliding down

the teapot's spout.

tEa

Or use the
teaspoon as an oar
to row a
sugar cube
to shore.

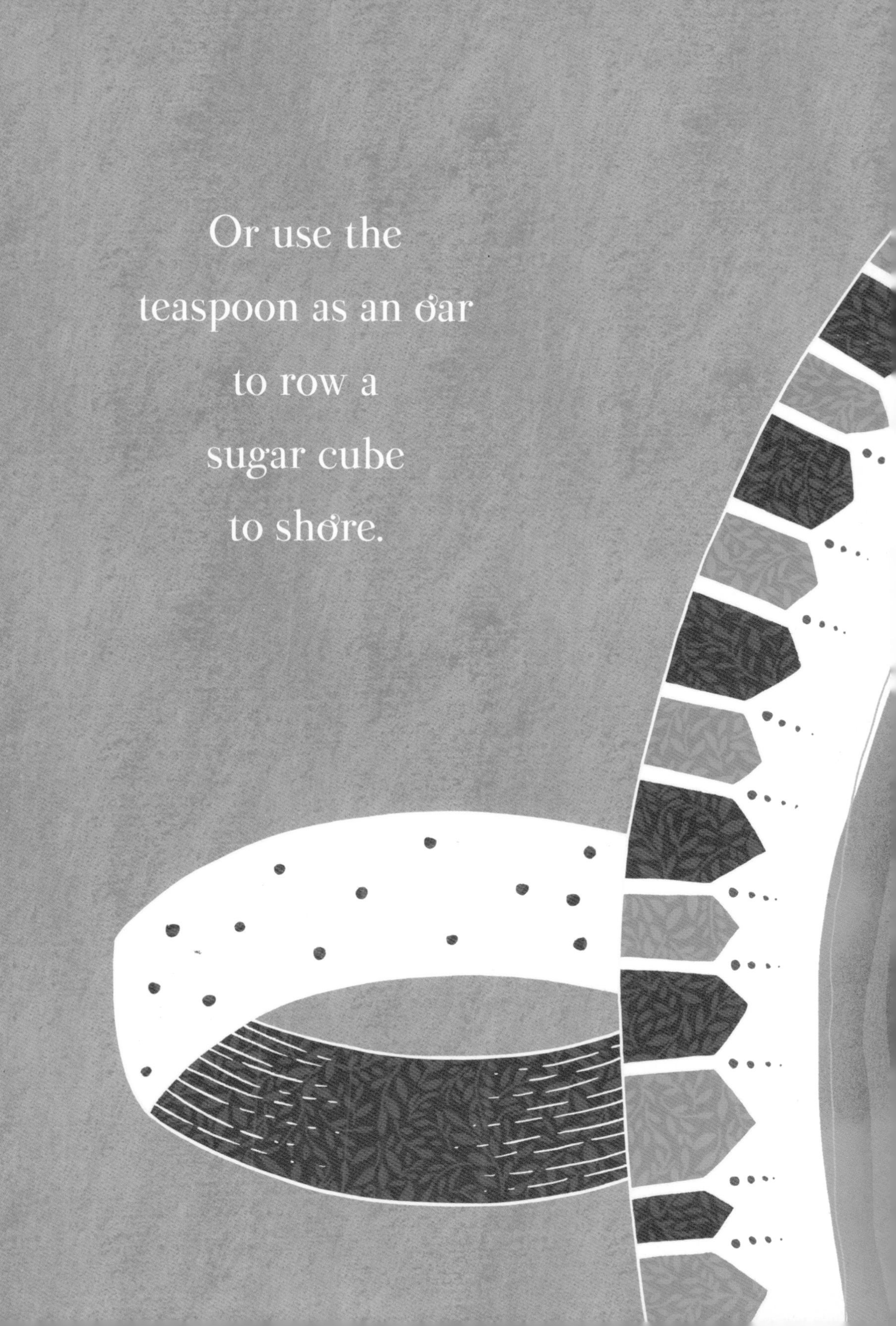

tea

The milky depths
lie unexplored.

–right off a teaspoon diving board.

So climb right in—or take a

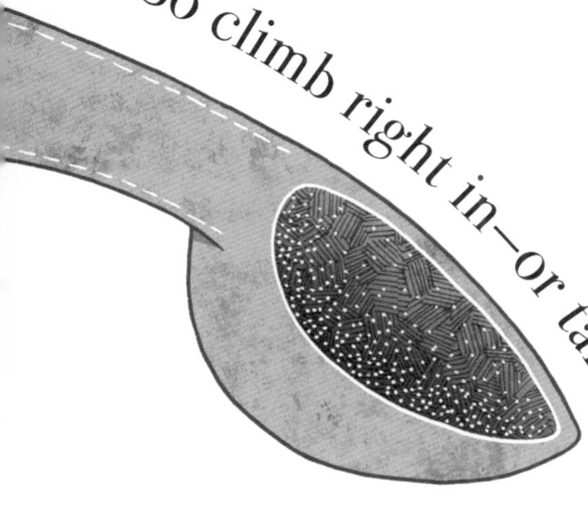

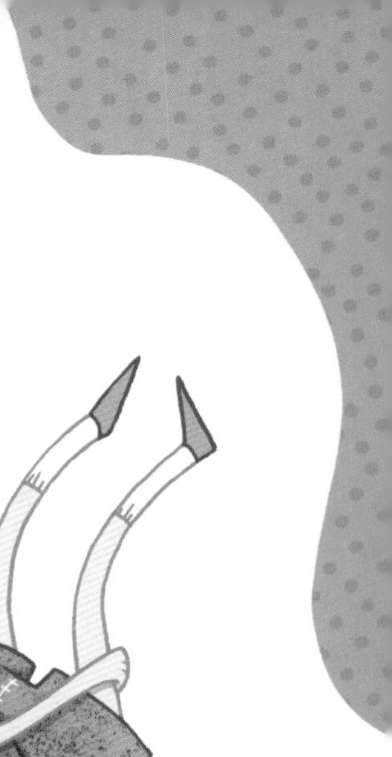

leap

It's not too hot

and nice

and

deep.

Please join me
in a cup of tea.
There's lots of room,
as you can see.

COOKIES
loose
tea
leaf

WRITTEN BY

Tiffany Stone

ILLUSTRATED BY

Jori van der Linde

SIMPLY READ BOOKS